E TAF
Tafuri, Nancy.
Silly little goose!

01

Best Books
Children's
Catalog

WITHDRAWN

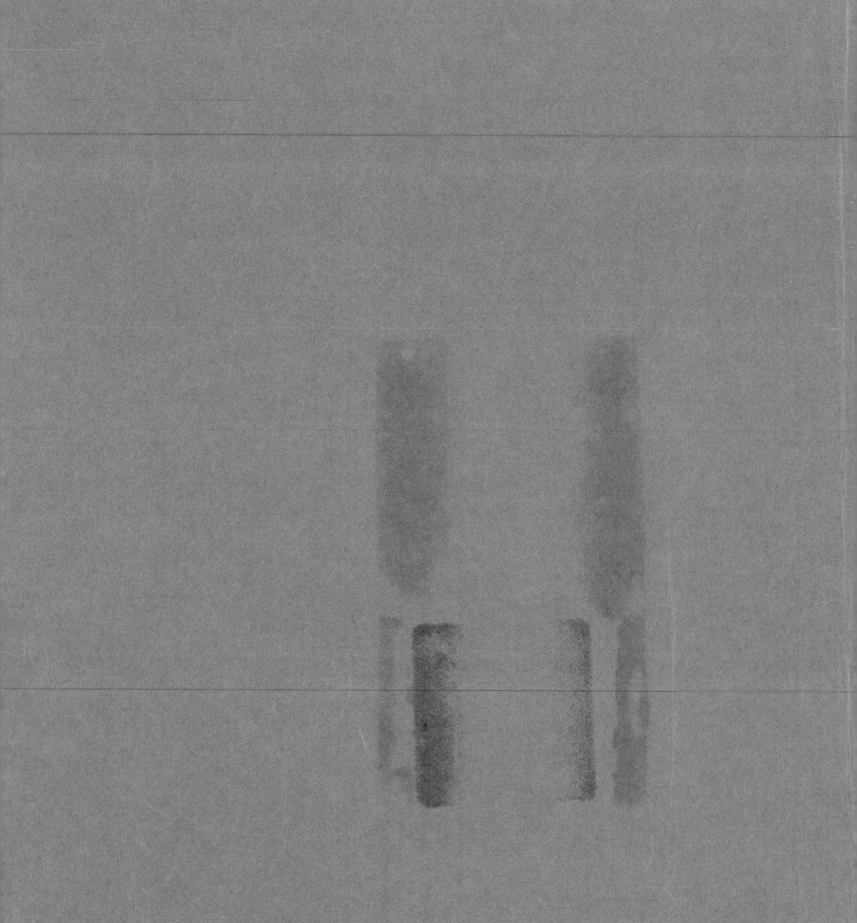

Silly Little Goose!

STORY AND PICTURES BY

Nancy Tafuri

Scholastic Press   New York

THE POND

THE CHICKEN HOUSE

THE SHEEP PEN

THE TOOLSHED

THE BIG BARN

Publishers since 1920. SCHOLASTIC and SCHOLASTIC PRESS and associated logos are trademarks and/or registered trademarks
of Scholastic Inc. Library of Congress Cataloging-in-Publication Data available. Library of Congress number: 00-025047
ISBN 0-439-06304-3   2 4 6 8 10 9 7 5 3 1   01 02 03 04 05
Book design by David Saylor   Printed in Mexico 49   First edition, April 2001

THE FIELD

THE FARMHOUSE

THE GARDEN

THE PIG YARD

• **To Cristina** •

One windy morning,
Goose sets out
to make a nest.

First, Goose finds

someplace nice and warm.

Next, Goose finds

someplace nice and soft.

mew! mew!

mew! mew!

SILLY LITTLE GOOSE!

Next, Goose finds

someplace nice and quiet.

BAAA!

SILLY
LITTLE
GOOSE!

Then Goose finds

someplace nice and cozy.

What's this?

It's warm.
It's soft.
It's quiet.
It's cozy.

It's perfect!

Goose makes her nest.
She lays her eggs.
She keeps them warm
for days and days. . .

until at last. . .

HOORAY FOR LITTLE GOOSE!

peep!

peep!

peep!

peep!

peep!

peep!

peep!